WOLF GIRL

For Safi, my very own wolf girl. My heart is
full of love for you and pride in you.
Mum xx

With special thanks to my nephew Brendan, whose tales
from the forests of Georgia, USA, sparked an idea.

Brimming with creative inspiration, how-to projects, and useful
information to enrich your everyday life, Quarto Knows is a favorite
destination for those pursuing their interests and passions. Visit our
site and dig deeper with our books into your area of interest:
Quarto Creates, Quarto Cooks, Quarto Homes, Quarto Lives,
Quarto Drives, Quarto Explores, Quarto Gifts, or Quarto Kids.

First published in the US in 2022 by Frances Lincoln Children's, an imprint of The Quarto Group.
100 Cummings Center, Suite 265D, Beverly, MA 01915, USA.
T +1 978-282-9590 F +1 078-283-2742 www.QuartoKnows.com

A CIP record for this book is available from the Library of Congress.
ISBN 978-0-7112-4957-8
eISBN 978-0-7112-7004-6

The illustrations were created using gouache paints.
Set in Truesdell and Foxhole
Published by Katie Cotton
Designed by Myrto Dimitrakoulia
Edited by Claire Grace
Production by Caragh McAleenan

Manufactured in Guangdong, China CC102021
1 3 5 7 9 8 6 4 2

MIX
Paper from
responsible sources
FSC® C008047
FSC
www.fsc.org

WOLF GIRL

JO LORING—FISHER

Frances Lincoln
Children's Books

Sophy watched the city from her window. Cars weaved and wound in endless spirals and twists, just like her worried tummy. The city was as gloomy and gray as she felt.

But inside was her DEN. Sophy was always happiest there.

She would put on her wolf suit and imagine she was …

FIERCE like a wolf.

FAST like a wolf.

STRONG like a wolf.

And maybe a little ˗BRAVE˗ like a wolf.

Sophy loved her wolf costume so much that she wished she could wear it to school.

So, one day she did. Sophy knew that everyone would like her
and want to be her friend when they saw her special wolf suit.

In the playground that day, Sophy plucked up the courage to talk to the other children.

But her words got stuck in her throat. And her head and tummy felt funny.

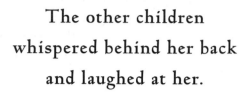

The other children
whispered behind her back
and laughed at her.

Sophy ran back home and curled into a little ball. She hugged herself as hot, salty tears streamed down her cheeks.

Then an EXTRAORDINARY thing happened.
Sophy felt an icy breeze on her face and she began to shake all over.

And SUDDENLY ...

... Sophy wasn't
alone anymore!

She had been joined by
a wolf and her pup.

And that wasn't all,
because all around her were
the silent, snowy woods she
knew from her books.

Sophy RAN

and ROLLED with the pup.

She PRANCED and HOWLED just like a wolf.

A huge smile spread across her face. She had made FRIENDS.

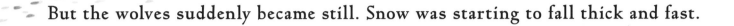

But the wolves suddenly became still. Snow was starting to fall thick and fast.

Feeling the biting wind, Sophy and the wolves headed for the woods.

Deeper and deeper they went, becoming colder and more exhausted until, at last, they found a cave.

They crouched together trying to get warm as the snowstorm roared outside.
But Sophy realized the roaring sound wasn't just coming from outside the cave.
It was inside, too. She looked up ...

... and saw an absolutely ENORMOUS BEAR!

Sophy was terrified. But deep inside she felt a
tingle and knew she had to be fierce, fast, strong,
and most importantly, BRAVE LIKE A WOLF.

The BEAR ran from the cave and out into the STORMY NIGHT.

Sophy smiled. She felt -BRAVE-
and it felt wonderful! The wolves
howled their praise and licked
and nuzzled her face.

But as a gust of snowy wind whistled through the cave, Sophy realized that the bear was
COLD and LONELY outside. Maybe he had just been looking for a place to shelter, like them.
He didn't look so big and scary any more. Sophy knew what she must do.

As Sophy walked outside, she
realized that sometimes being KIND
was the BRAVEST thing of all.

As they all HUDDLED together, Sophy realized
that she felt quite different. She had friends, and she
liked that feeling very much. An owl hooted softly
outside and Sophy fell fast asleep.

Sophy opened her eyes and
realized she was back in her den
and alone once more. "Had it all
been a dream?" she wondered sadly.

But then she remembered that feeling of BRAVERY and WARMTH and realized it was still inside her.

She carried that feeling with her into school. She held onto it when someone asked her to join in. And this time her words didn't get stuck in her throat and she replied in her quiet way,

"YES PLEASE."

Sophy carried her brave feeling inside all day.

And later on, Sophy spotted an OWLISH LITTLE BOY.

The one whom no one ever noticed. They shared a shy smile and Sophy knew she had made a FRIEND.